Usborne First Experiences

Moving house

Anne Civardi
Illustrated by Stephen Cartwright

Consultant: Betty Root

There is a little yellow duck hiding on every two pages. Can you find it?

The Sparks

SOPHIE SPARK

PATCH

DAD SPARK

MUM SPARK

SAM SPARK

PETER

PLOD

This is the Spark family. Sam is seven and Sophie is five.
They are moving into a new house soon.

The old house

This is their old house. The Sparks sold it to Mr. and Mrs. Potts. The Potts have come to tea today.

At the new house

The next day, the Sparks go to see their new house. It needs painting before they can move in.

Two men from Cosy Carpets have arrived to put new carpets down in some of the rooms.

Packing up

It takes Mum and Dad many days to sort out and pack up all their things. Packing is hard work.

Sam makes sure his things are packed too. But Sophie would rather play than pack.

On the move

Today is moving day. Early in the morning, the removal people arrive to help the Sparks.

Bill, Frank and Bess load everything into their big removal van and drive it to the new house.

Unloading the van

Bill shows Sam and Sophie the inside of the van. Then they all go to the new house and help unload.

Bill, Frank and Bess carry the heavy furniture into the house. Mum shows them where to put it.

Sophie's new bedroom

Dad helps Sophie get her new bedroom ready. She is very excited about moving house.

Sam's new bedroom

Sam has his own room too. He likes the new house.
Now he does not have to share a room with Sophie.

The new neighbours

In the afternoon, the Sparks meet their neighbours.
Lots of children live nearby.

Sophie and Sam will have new friends to play with.
Mrs. Tobbit gives Dad a big cake to welcome them.

The first night

Sophie, Sam, Mum and Dad are very tired after the move. They are fast asleep in their new home.

First published in 1985. This enlarged edition first published in 1992. Usborne Publishing Ltd, 83-85 Saffron Hill, London EC1N 8RT, England. © Usborne Publishing Ltd, 1992.